1
GAPING
WIDE-MOUTHED
HOPPING FROG

Atheneum
8166 Third
N.Y. N.Y.

MAIL

Books by
LESLIE TRYON

Albert's Alphabet

Albert's Play

Toohy and Wood
(*written by Mary Elise Monsell*)

1
GAPING
WIDE-MOUTHED
HOPPING FROG

LESLIE TRYON

ATHENEUM 1993 NEW YORK

Maxwell Macmillan Canada
Toronto
Maxwell Macmillan International
New York   Oxford   Singapore   Sydney

Special thanks to Con, Carole,
Sir Cedric, and Gracie.

Atheneum
Macmillan Publishing Company
866 Third Avenue
New York, NY 10022

Maxwell Macmillan Canada, Inc.
1200 Eglinton Avenue East
Suite 200
Don Mills, Ontario M3C 3N1

Macmillan Publishing Company is part of the
Maxwell Communication Group of Companies.

First edition
Printed in Hong Kong by
South China Printing Company (1988) Ltd.
10 9 8 7 6 5 4 3 2 1
The text of this book is set in 22 point Caslon 224 Medium.
The illustrations are rendered in watercolors, pen and ink, and Prismacolor pencils.

Library of Congress Cataloging-in-Publication Data
Tryon, Leslie.
One gaping wide-mouthed hopping frog / by Leslie Tryon. — 1st ed.
p.   cm.
Summary: Hopping Frog, the mail carrier, takes the reader along
his route through a village bustling with activity in this counting rhyme.
ISBN 0-689-31785-9
1. Nursery rhymes.   2. Children's poetry.   [1. Nursery rhymes.
2. Counting.   3. Frogs—Poetry.]   I. Title.
PZ8.3.T77On   1993
398.8—dc20   92-11368

1 gaping wide–mouthed hopping frog,

2 birthday cakes for a very old dog,

3 monkeys dancing the clog,

 ostriches who like to jog,

5 puppies so tiny and small,
who daily for their breakfast call.

5 puppies so tiny and small,
   who daily for their breakfast call.

4 ostriches who like to jog,

3 monkeys dancing the clog,

2 birthday cakes for a very old dog, and . . .

1 gaping wide–mouthed hopping frog.

6 beetles crawl up the wall

of Gracie's Apple Magic Stall.

7 lobsters in a dish

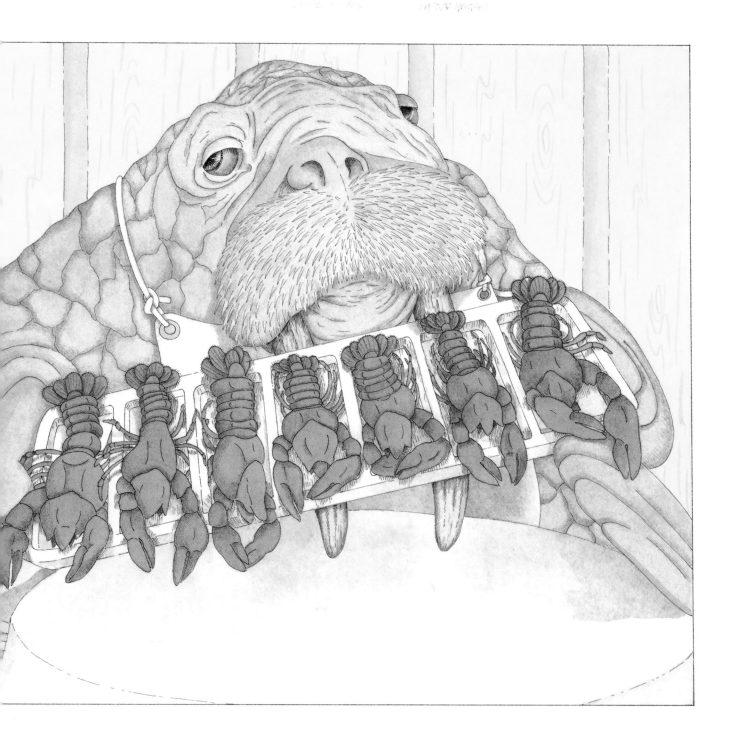

for a walrus fond of fish.

8 joiners on a joiners hall

working in their overalls.

9 children on the bus

each one waving back at us.

10
peacocks in the air—

how long will they stay up there?

10

9

8

7

6

5

4

3

2 🎂🎂 **and...**

1 gaping wide-mouthed hopping frog.

10 peacocks in the air—
how long will they stay up there?
9 children on the bus
each one waving back at us.
8 joiners on a joiners hall
working in their overalls.
7 lobsters in a dish
for a walrus fond of fish.
6 beetles crawl up the wall
of Gracie's Apple Magic Stall.
5 puppies so tiny and small,
who daily for their breakfast call.
4 ostriches who like to jog,
3 monkeys dancing the clog,
2 birthday cakes for a very old dog,
and . . .
1 gaping wide–mouthed hopping frog.